ALFIE's
Feet

For Edward and Catherine

Other books about Alfie:

Alfie Gets in First

Alfie Gives a Hand

An Evening at Alfie's

Alfie and the Birthday Surprise

Alfie Wins a Prize

Alfie Weather

Annie Rose is my Little Sister

The Big Alfie and Annie Rose Storybook

The Big Alfie Out of Doors Storybook

Rhymes for Annie Rose

Alfie's Alphabet

Alfie's Numbers

ALFIE'S FEET
A RED FOX BOOK 0 09 925606 1
First published in Great Britain by The Bodley Head,
an imprint of Random House Children's Books
The Bodley Head edition published 1982
This Red Fox edition published 2004
9 11 13 12 10 8
Copyright © Shirley Hughes, 1982
The right of Shirley Hughes to be identified as the author and illustrator of this work
has been asserted in accordance with the Copyright, Designs and Patents Act 1988.
All rights reserved.
Red Fox Books are published by Random House Children's Books,
61–63 Uxbridge Road, London W5 5SA,
a division of The Random House Group Ltd,
in Australia by Random House Australia (Pty) Ltd,
20 Alfred Street, Milsons Point, Sydney, NSW 2061, Australia,
in New Zealand by Random House New Zealand Ltd,
18 Poland Road, Glenfield, Auckland 10, New Zealand,
and in South Africa by Random House (Pty) Ltd,
Endulini, 5A Jubilee Road, Parktown 2193, South Africa
THE RANDOM HOUSE GROUP Limited Reg. No. 954009
www.kidsatrandomhouse.co.uk
A CIP catalogue record for this book is available from the British Library.
Printed in China

ALFIE's Feet

Shirley Hughes

RED FOX

This little pig went to market,

This little pig stayed at home,

This little pig had roast beef,

This little pig had none,

And this little pig cried, Wee-wee-wee-wee-wee,

I can't find my way home.

Alfie had a little sister called Annie Rose. Alfie's feet were quite big. Annie Rose's feet were rather small. They were all soft and pink underneath. Alfie knew a game he could play with Annie Rose, counting her toes.

Annie Rose had lots of different
ways of getting about. She went
forwards, crawling,

and backwards, on her behind,

and she liked to slide
about very fast on her potty,

skidding round and round
on the floor and in and out
of the table legs.

Annie Rose had
some new red shoes.

She could walk in them
a bit, if she was pushing her
little cart or holding on to
someone's hand.

When they went out, Annie Rose wore her
red shoes and Alfie wore his old brown ones.
Mum usually helped him put them on, because
he wasn't very good at doing up the laces yet.

If it had been raining Alfie
liked to go stamping about in
mud and walking through puddles,

splish, splash, SPLOSH!

Then his shoes got rather wet.

So did his socks,

and so did his feet.

So one Saturday morning Alfie and Mum went to a big shop in the High Street.

They bought a pair of shiny new yellow boots for Alfie to wear when he went stamping about in mud and walking through puddles. Alfie was very pleased. He carried them home himself in a cardboard box.

When they got in, Alfie sat down at
once and unwrapped his new boots. He
put them on all by himself and walked
about in them,

stamp! stamp! stamp!

He went into the kitchen to show Mum and Dad
and Annie Rose, stamping his feet all the way,

stamp! stamp! stamp!

The boots were very smart
and shiny but they felt funny.

Alfie wanted to go out again right away. So he put on his mac, and Dad took his book and his newspaper and they went off to the park.

Alfie stamped in a lot of mud and walked through a lot of puddles, splish, splash, SPLOSH! He frightened some sparrows who were having a bath. He even frightened two big ducks. They went hurrying back to their pond, walking with their feet turned in.

Alfie looked down at his feet. They still
felt funny. They kept turning outwards.
Dad was sitting on a bench. They both
looked at Alfie's feet.

Suddenly Alfie knew what was wrong!

Dad lifted Alfie on to the bench beside him and helped him to take off each boot and put it on the other foot. And when Alfie stood down again his feet didn't feel a bit funny any more.

After tea Mum painted a big black R on to one of Alfie's boots and a big black L on the other to help Alfie remember which boot was which. The R was for Right foot and the L was for Left foot. The black paint wore off in the end and the boots stopped being new and shiny, but Alfie usually did remember to get them on the proper way round after that. They felt much better when he went stamping about in mud and walking through puddles.

And, of course, Annie Rose made such a fuss about Alfie having new boots that she had to have a pair of her own to go stamping about in too, splish, splash, SPLOSH!